CURTAIN CALL

Games, Skits, Plays & More

by

Elizabeth Koehler-Pentacoff

Incentive Publications, Inc.
Nashville, Tennessee

Cover by Susan Eaddy
Illustrated by Susan Eaddy
Edited by Sally Sharpe

ISBN 0-86530-065-8

Table of Contents

PREFACE

Drama is fun, fosters self-esteem and group cooperation, increases self-discipline and concentration, and encourages creative self-expression. Creative drama activities provide children with highly motivational learning experiences through which the children learn by "becoming." This exciting, natural approach to learning will encourage children to explore and develop their talents and capabilities.

CURTAIN CALL was created for teachers, children's librarians, scout and recreation leaders, camp counselors, parents, and anyone wanting to provide children with exciting and stimulating creative expression activities and drama opportunities. The book is divided into eight thematic chapters to help you quickly and easily find activities, games, skits and plays for many different occasions.

All of the games require only readily-accessible "equipment" and are extremely easy to lead. They may be used as five-minute fillers, rainy day recess (or sunny day recess!), fun "breaks" from daily routine, birthday party games, and home entertainment. Once children have played a game, they may play it again and again without adult instruction. The games are varied enough for any age level — even adults will enjoy them!

In addition to games, skits and storytelling activities are included to foster creative thinking skills, spontaneity, and verbal expression as well as to supplement literature and library programs and initiate general acting enthusiasm! Children will delight in creating original commercials, funny tales, and newspaper headline skits.

For those who are looking for children's plays or find themselves in charge of putting on a play, three familiar fairy tales are written in play form and are ready to be reproduced and used in staging instant productions. What's more, a complete chapter is devoted to information related to "putting on a play" and includes tips for selecting and writing plays and "notes to the director" concerning play production. Other useful material such as reproducible forms, stage areas and terms, and cues for actors and directors may be found in the appendix.

SENSATIONAL SENSES

Sensory Exploration

...Band-Aid on knee...

...green sweatshirt

BACK TO BACK

Have partners stand facing each other. When the signal "back to back" is given, students should turn around and take turns describing one another's clothing and general appearance. Then each student should make two changes in his or her appearance such as untieing a shoe, taking off a watch, or rolling up a sleeve. After making the changes, the partners should face each other and try to identify the changes made.

TAPE RECORDED AUTOBIOGRAPHY

Instruct partners to take turns telling each other about themselves. While one student is talking, the other student may not say a word. Topics may include hobbies, families, pets, favorite foods, books, television shows, etc. Each autobiography should take one minute. When the minute is up, the talking partner must stop and the listening partner (the "tape recorder") must repeat what he or she remembers (for one minute only). Then the partners may discuss the experience for one minute after which the second autobiography is told and "recorded."

PAPER FOLD

Have each student choose a partner. Instruct the partners to sit with their backs together. Give each student a piece of paper — one of the papers should be folded in several different ways and the other paper should not be folded. The student with the folded paper must try to tell the other student how to fold his or her paper so that the two papers will be identical.

I'M GOING ON A PICNIC

Have the group sit in a circle. Choose a leader and instruct the leader to begin the game by saying, "My name is __Liz__. I'm going on a picnic and I will take . . . __a kite__." The next person must tell what the leader is taking and then add his or her name and an object. For example: "__Liz__ is taking __a kite__. My name is __Sally__. I'm going on a picnic and I will take __a radio__." Each student must tell what the people before him or her are taking and then add his or her name and an object. If someone forgets a name or an object or changes the order, that person is out of the game.

11

BLINDFOLD WALK

we're coming to the big tree on the playground

Let partners take turns blindfolding one another. One partner must lead the blindfolded partner around the room. (The object is to assist, not to trick.) The "seeing" partner should accurately describe the surroundings. For example: "We are coming to the stairs. Take three steps and then feel the stairs with your foot." After the partners have explored the room or outside yard, they may trade roles.

MYSTERY BAG

Blindfold the students and have them use their senses to identify objects.

Touch: feather, balloon, shell, sandpaper, fur, money

Smell: coffee, perfume, rubbing alcohol, onion

Taste: raisins, cornflakes, coconut, crackers, marshmallows, chocolate

SENSE THE SOUND

Ask all of the students to close their eyes. Have one group member make a noise somewhere in the room. The other students must determine where the sound is coming from and how it is being made. (Examples: writing on the chalkboard, opening the curtains, closing a window or door, using hands to make the sound of pounding horses' hooves, making a train whistle noise, tapping fingers to make the sound of rain, etc.)

WHAT DID YOU SEE?

Place various objects on a tray for everyone to view. Then cover the tray and ask the students to name the items they remember seeing on the tray.

WHO STARTED THE MOTION?

Have the group sit in a circle. Ask one student to leave the room. Choose a leader. The leader is to begin making a motion and the others are to imitate the leader. Ask the student who left the room to enter, to stand in the middle of the circle, and to try to determine who the leader is. The leader should occasionally change the motion and the others should follow as quickly as possible so as not to give away the leader's identity. (Remind the students to look straight across the circle and not at the leader.) The game continues as students take turns acting as the leader and the one chosen to leave the room.

WHERE ARE THE CLOTHESPINS?

Ask the students to close their eyes while you place two clothespins on the clothing of two students. Be sure to place the clothespins where they may be seen — on pockets, shirt collars, shoelaces, or even in hair. Instruct the students to walk around the room and look for the clothespins without talking to or touching anyone. The students "wearing" the clothespins should act as though they do not have them and should "search" with the others. When a student spots a clothespin, he or she must "die" (fall down). (Students should not "die" near the clothespin carriers.) The last two students to spot the clothespins become the next clothespin carriers.

CANDY GAME

Choose a leader and instruct the leader to pretend to be a candy vendor. The other students should pretend to hear the vendor, see the vendor, and buy the vendor's candy. The students may unwrap the candy, smell it, and then eat it. Types of candy to taste might include sour drops, chocolate, sticky taffy, and crunchy peanut brittle.

After the activity, discuss these questions:

1. Do the facial expressions change with the various candies?
2. How do the tastes of the candies differ?

FANTASTIC FEET

Have the students take off their shoes and socks and feel different materials using only their feet! Good materials of different textures include mud, sand, flour, and water. (Spread newspaper on the floor or do this activity outside!)

RELAXATION STIMULATION

Ask the students to relax and explore their five senses by pretending to . . .

Touch . . .
   a hot stove
   icicles
   sharp tacks
   velvet

Smell . . .
   freshly baked bread
   a skunk
   perfume
   onions

Taste . . .
   a sour lemon
   your favorite candy
   spinach

Hear . . .
   a gentle wind
   a loud whistle
   a distant train
   underwater sounds

See . . .
   a car far away, coming towards you
   a giant
   an ant

THE SOUNDS OF MUSIC

Music, Movement,

Rhythm And Sound

STREAMERS DANCE

For this activity, use waltz music or other "slow" music so that the movements will be graceful and not jumpy. Each dancer will need one or two colored streamers. The dancers may move to the music individually at first and then work with partners to create original dances. (The students might like to name their dances!) For a variation, dancers may stand in a circle and perform together.

DRUM, DRUM, DRUM

Play Sandy Nelson's "Let There Be Drums" and ask each student to pretend that he or she is a famous drummer. As the record begins, there is only one drum. Narrate as more drums and cymbals are introduced.

Example:
"Drums are above your head! On the floor! Behind you! In front of you! Don't forget the cymbals and the foot drums!"

Let There Be Drums, Capitol Records, 1961.

MOVE TO THE BEAT

Have the group form a circle. Pass the ball around the circle to the beat of a drum . . . or have the students walk, crawl or climb an imaginary ladder to drumbeats.

CHARACTER CHANGE

Use drumbeats as character signals. For example, one beat of the drum signals everyone to turn into cats. Two beats of the drum signal everyone to change into dogs. Three beats of the drum signal everyone to turn into birds, etc.

MOVING TO MUSIC

Circus
Play circus music and watch the students become clowns, trapeze artists, animals, animal trainers, and other circus characters!

Ragtime Music
Ragtime music "sets the stage" for silent films. Students will enjoy acting out their own silent films. Broad acting, exaggeration, and no dialogue are perfect for slapstick-style humor.

Space Music
Students will enjoy "exploring" space and the earth as they listen to space music.

SOUND STORY

Let students take turns being the narrator and telling a story while the rest of the group create the sound effects. By raising or lowering his or her hand, the narrator may control the volume. When the narrator's hand is high in the air, the sound effects should be loud. When the narrator's hand touches the floor, all should be quiet. As the narrator's hand rises, the volume should increase. Good story topics include taking a boat ride during a storm, visiting a zoo at feeding time, and going to a haunted house on Halloween night.

SOUND CHORUS

Have the students position themselves as though they are about to sing in a choir. Assign an emotion to each student such as bashfulness, hysteria, anger, happiness, fear, sadness, impatience, etc. The student must think of a facial expression and/or body movement and a sound to symbolize his or her emotion. This activity works equally as well for other topics: seasons of the year, foods (liver, spaghetti, ice cream and Jell-O are good), places (Niagra Falls, New York City, Hollywood, etc.), animals (a frog with hiccups, a turtle in a race, etc.), objects (a dripping faucet, a squeaky door, etc.), and even diseases (chicken pox, mumps, etc.).

SOUND OBSTACLE COURSE

Set up an obstacle course using chairs, tables, boxes, and other objects. Attach a sign which has a specific sound written on it to each obstacle. As students come to each obstacle, they must make the specified sound. For example, when a student climbs over a chair, he or she must make the sound of a car horn. When the student climbs under a table, he or she must make thunderstorm noises. As students complete the course, they may position themselves to "become" part of the obstacle course itself!

SOUND CREATION

Students will enjoy creating the following sounds:

whistle

scratch

zip

snore

whisper

flutter

crunch

slam

smack

slide				
drip	roll			
drop	blast	hum	pop	thud
boom	splash	snap	sizzle	crash
shatter	bang	crack	buzz	scrape
		crackle	tap	swish

22

THE MAGIC OF MIME

Pantomiming

PERSONAL SPACE BUBBLES

Tell the students that everyone has his or her own "personal space bubble." Hold out your arms to illustrate the personal space bubble around you. Then ask the students to stand up and hold out their arms to define their own personal space bubbles. Explain that when the students are "in" their personal space bubbles, they are not to touch anyone or anything and should not have eye contact with anyone except you.

Let the students experience the following activities in their personal space bubbles!

Shake Out

Give instructions to the students for moving specific body parts. Have the students "shake out" each body part and move some body parts simultaneously.

Example:
"Shake out your right hand. Now shake out your whole arm. Shake out your left foot . . . wiggle those toes!"

Walk, Walk, Walk

Ask the students to walk . . .
- with the beat of the drum
- on snails
- through tall grass
- on hot pavement
- on ice cubes
- as soldiers
- as space people
- as apes
- as kings or queens

Move To The Beat
Instruct the students to fall to the ground and get up as quickly as possible when they hear a drumbeat. Then ask the students to fall down and get up to the beat of the drum.

Believing Is Becoming
Tell the students to become . . .
- a bubble floating in the sky
- a puppet
- a caterpillar crawling on a branch
- a clock
- a windshield wiper

Time To Change
This activity will allow students to explore the process of change. Ask each student to be . . .
- a withering flower
- uncooked spaghetti noodles becoming soft, cooked spaghetti noodles
- jeans in a washing machine . . . and then jeans on a clothesline
- frozen ice cream placed in the hot sun

Relax!

Ask the students to relax and to . . .

- be a snowman on a sunny day
- grow into a horrible, ugly monster that eats trees

- become a floating balloon
- change from a lovely young sapling into a weathered old tree
- be a blade of grass blowing in the wind
- walk along a very high tightrope

- drift like a piece of driftwood in the water
- be an autumn leaf tumbling to the ground
- walk through the jungle like an elephant
- be a baby taking its first few steps

- swing from the trees like a monkey
- become a big grizzly bear scratching its back on the bark of a tree
- waddle across an iceberg like a penguin
- fan your feathers and strut like a peacock
- tumble down a high, high hill
- be a tropical fish swimming in the ocean

OH UP, OH DOWN

This game is a perfect "personal space bubble" activity. The leader raises his or her hands high above the head and says, "Oh up." The group then stands up and repeats, "Oh up." Then the leader crouches to the floor and says, "Oh down." The students follow by crouching to the floor and repeating, "Oh down." Then the leader says, "When you stand up, be a _____ ."

The students may make sound effects and use pantomime to act out the part. Choose from the following suggestions or make up other "parts" of your own for the students to pantomime.

Suggestions:
- animals, farm or zoo
- melting snowman
- rag doll
- toaster
- career persons (dentist, teacher, lion tamer, etc.)
- witch
- clown
- a drowning dragon
- a bawling baby

SCRAPBOOK

Choose a student to be the leader. Instruct the leader to narrate a story and the group to pantomime the narration. When the leader yells, "Picture!", the group should freeze in whatever positions they are in to "make a picture" for the scrapbook they are creating. Possible story ideas include taking a camping trip; going to the zoo, park or carnival; taking a boat outing or visiting a big city.

ANYONE FOR CHARADES?

Students always enjoy a good old fashioned game of charades! Have the students pantomime titles of movies, television shows, books or songs. Prepare title cards in advance or let the students come up with their own titles. (Consult the library for help.) Before beginning each charade, the player must give signals as to what type of title he or she will pantomime. Other signals (below) will give the students additional help.

Signals:
- movie · wind a movie camera
- T.V. show · outline a T.V. screen
- book · form an open book with hands
- song · open mouth and pretend to hold a microphone
- little word · hold thumb and index finger close together for words such as *a*, *the*, *to*, and *as*
- number of words · hold up fingers to show total number of words and then to show which word will be pantomimed first
- syllables · extend one forearm and place fingers of other hand on the extended arm to show the number of syllables

MIGHTY MAGNET

Divide the students into two teams. Have the teams line up as in a relay race. Tell the students that there is an imaginary magnet at the opposite end of the room which "attracts" students in pairs. As students are drawn to the magnet, they should try to resist the powerful force. Give instructions such as, "The magnet is pulling you by your head . . . by your bellybutton . . . by your nose . . . etc."

ALPHABET GAME

Have the group form a circle and instruct them to act out letters of the alphabet. The first student should act out something that begins with the letter "a" (eating an *apple*, becoming an *ape* or *alligator*, etc.). The other students should mimick the pantomime. The second student must act out the letter "b" (playing *baseball* or eating a *banana*, etc.). Again, the group should mimick the pantomime. The game continues until the alphabet has been completed.

(Helpful hint: x · playing the *xylophone!*)

A is for Ape

MY FRIEND HERBIE

Tell the students that you have a very special friend you would like them to meet. Then reach into your pocket and pull out a tiny imaginary friend. Say something such as the following: "Meet my friend Herbie. Herbie is so small that you can't see him unless you have a powerful microscope. As I pass Herbie to each of you, he will grow in size. Each time he is passed from hand to hand, he will get larger and heavier. By the time Herbie reaches the last person, he will be huge! Then we will pass Herbie around again so that he will slowly shrink to his original size." Discuss size, shape, weight and proportion. Make sure that Herbie doesn't grow from tiny to huge in one pass!

STATUES

Have the students stand in a circle and walk clockwise. Instruct the leader to stand in the center of the circle and to say, "Statue man, statue man, make me a statue as fast as you can." Then the leader chooses one person and spins him or her around once. When the person stops spinning, he or she is to freeze in a position and become a statue. After everyone has been "frozen" into a statue, the leader pushes a magic button to bring the statues to life. Let the students take turns being the leader.

OBJECT CREATION

Direct groups of three to seven students to form objects that move and make noise. Each student in the group must be used to create or operate the machine.

For example, a lawn mower can be made by using four people as wheels, one person for the body, and one person for the handle. One student can push the mower and all of the students can participate in creating the sound effects. Suggestions for other objects to create include an eggbeater, record player, garbage disposal, toaster, washing machine, pencil sharpener, water fountain, coffee pot, fire extinguisher, computer, vacuum cleaner, typewriter, microwave, popcorn popper, and calculator.

YARDSTICK PANTOMIME

Have the group stand in a circle. Let one student at a time use a yardstick in a pantomime. For example, a student could pantomime hitting a baseball with a bat. The other students should try to guess what object the yardstick is supposed to be. Ideas for possible "objects" to be pantomimed include musical instruments, objects to be used in school or around the house or yard, sporting equipment, etc.

SHARE THE WORK!

Instruct pairs of students to "work at something" with an imaginary object between them (spread a sheet, pull taffy, etc.). The first exercise may be done with hands. Then have the students clasp their hands behind their backs as they reenact the same scenes.

WHAT'S THE PROBLEM?

Have small groups of students pantomime scenes in which an object becomes the major problem of the scene. For example, students could struggle with a pull-down bed, try to open the window to a fire escape, or attempt to open a stuck closet door!

HELP! I CAN'T GET OUT!

Ask each student to pantomime a situation in which he or she can't get out of an entanglement. For example, a student could become "involved" with a boa constrictor, a spider web, a fishing net, a parachute, etc. Concentration should be on the object, not on the entanglement.

LET'S GO ON A TRIP

Have the group pretend that they are on an object that is moving such as a sailboat, a train, a merry-go-round, a Ferris wheel, etc.

I'M A TEAPOT

Instruct the students to work in pairs. One student should become an object and the other student should "use" that object. Examples for objects include a piano, a broom, a footstool, and a revolving door.

MACHINE CREATION

Ask each student to think about something he or she hates to do. Then instruct the students to "create" machines to do those tasks for them! Let the students demonstrate their machines before the group.

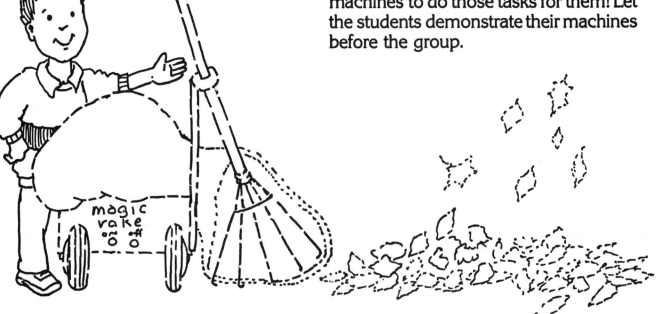

TALENTED IMPOSTORS

Role Playing
And Character Development

MUSICAL HATS

Place a hat on a chair for each student. Play music while the students walk around the chairs. When the music stops, each student is to grab a hat from a chair and sit down in that chair. Then the student is to put on the hat and "become" the person who would wear that hat. (Good hats to use include a clown, witch, police officer, firefighter, cowboy or cowgirl, and Santa Claus hat.) To adapt this game for older students, tape signs with character names to the chairs. Each student is to become the character whose name is on the chair in which he or she sits.

WHO AM I?

Pin a sign having the name of a character or famous person written on it on each student's back. Instruct the students to move around the room asking classmates yes or no questions in order to determine who they are. Choose characters such as those below:

- Cartoon Characters - Mickey Mouse, Donald Duck, Fred Flinstone, Bugs Bunny, etc.
- Fantasy Figures - the Easter Bunny, the Great Pumpkin, the Tooth Fairy, etc.
- Celebrities - famous actors, actresses and singers; famous historical figures; etc.

ANIMAL PARADE

Let each student choose what animal he or she would like to be in the class animal parade. Suggest animals such as a big, lazy cow, a noisy hen, a slithering rattlesnake, a timid mouse, a sleepy turtle, a waddling duck, and a playful puppy. Have the students practice moving as their chosen animals and making the appropriate sound effects. Stage an animal parade! After the parade, ask each "animal" to act out various situations: the animal is hungrily eating supper, the animal gets caught in a large web or trap, the animal finds itself lost in a strange place, etc.

BUS STOP/ELEVATOR

Write a character description on an index card for each student. Then let each student pick a card from the stack and "become" the character on that card. Explain that all of the characters are either waiting for a bus or are stuck in an elevator. None of the characters may say who he or she is. Instruct the characters to interact with one another as they "act" to determine everyone's identity.

Character Suggestions:
> a washer woman going home after work, a maniac, a famous actor or actress, an immigrant who doesn't speak English, a teacher, an escaped convict, a politician, etc.

PRETZEL

Ask one student to leave the room and have the other students join hands to form a circle. Instruct the students to twist and turn until they are told to freeze. Remind the students not to let go so that the pretzel will not break! Then let the student who has left the room return and tell the others how to untangle themselves. Directions must be clear.

● Wrong: "Move your arm up and turn."
● Right: "Move your left arm over your head and turn to the right."

MASKS

Have the students form a circle. Instruct one student to create an emotional expression on his or her face. The student should then peel off the mask, working from the forehead to the chin. Instruct the student to throw the mask to another student who should "put on" the mask and try to immitate the expression. The student then peels off the mask and creates a new face which is passed to another student in the same manner. The game continues until all have had a turn.

THREE-GENERATION PHOTO

Divide the students into groups of three each. Instruct each student in the group to take on the role of a child, parent or grandparent. Have the students in each group act out their roles and then "pose" for a three-generation photo!

PAIRS IN CONFLICT

Let students work in pairs to act out a conflict such as a parent and teenager discussing curfew, a salesperson and customer talking about the price of an item, etc. Remind the students that shouting or physical contact is not allowed. Then have the partners trade roles. Instruct the students to plan their strategies and to determine how compromises might be reached.

Use these fun exercises to teach students good articulation!

Jaw Stretch
Instruct each student to pretend that he or she has a triple decker sandwich in his or her hands. Give the signal for the student to take a BIG BITE and then chew!

Pronunciation Exaggeration
Form a circle. Let each student "pronounce" each phrase below. Choose one phrase at a time, letting each student in the circle say that phrase before going on to the next one. Remind the students not to swallow the final consonants but to stress them!

- A · E · I · O · U
- Will you wait for Willie?
- The cream-colored cat crept into the crib and crept out again.
- Eniemeanie pinch a meanie.
- Butta gutta butta gutta (NOT budda!)
- Hello, my name is _____ .
- Tick-a tick-a tick-a tick-a (faster and faster!)
- She sells seashells by the seashore.

IMAGINATION IN ACTION

Improvisation

DUBBING

Have one group of students act out a scene and another group of students stand "behind the stage" (or off to the side) and create the voices!

Ooohhh, pleeease... Won't you forgive me for trying to teach your cat to swim?

SHADOWS

Let two students plan and present a brief skit for one of the suggested scenes below. Ask another pair of students to "shadow" the movements of the actors and to make remarks to the audience. The actors are to ignore the "shadowers" and are to pretend that nothing unusual is happening.

Suggested Scenes:
- teacher and student in class
- customer and salesperson in a store
- two people at a party
- two people eating at a restaurant
- brother and sister at home
- two people sitting beside each other on the bus

ROBOT DRAMA

Briefly discuss what it would be like to be a robot. Ask questions such as: "What would a robot eat?" "What would a robot do for fun?" "How would robots from another planet react to our way of life and how would we react to them?" Have a group of students present a skit in which they walk and talk like robots. The students may choose to have one "human" in the scene for contrast.

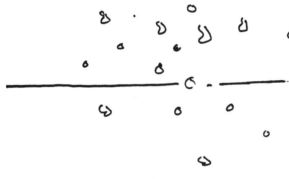

HILARIOUS HANDS

Let the students work in groups of four for this activity. Instruct the students to plan "scenes" involving a lot of hand movements such as eating at a restaurant, putting something together, etc. Two of the students in each group are to stand side by side with their hands behind their backs. They will provide the voices and facial expressions. The other two students in the group are to stand behind the pair and extend their arms around the students to be the "hands." The students in front are not to move so that the audience will see only the hands of the hidden students. Let one group at a time present its scene before the class.

43

DOMINOES

Have two students begin a skit. When each student has established his or her character, let another student tap one of the players on the shoulder and step in to take his or her place. The new player must resume the exact body position of the person leaving the scene and must begin a different skit from that position. The "old" player must join in until another student taps him or her on the shoulder.

Example:
A and B are playing basketball. C steps in for A (if A has been in longer) and takes the position of A who was shooting a basket. C uses that motion to pretend that he is lifting a heavy box onto a shelf. B assists C. Then D steps in for B and begins another skit.

THEMATIC DOMINOES

oops! I thought you were an elevator button.

No! I'm Buttons the clown!

Follow the instructions above for "Dominoes" with this exception: all of the skits must have one specific theme.

Example:
Buttons - sewing on a button, pushing an elevator button, talking to or about a clown named Buttons, looking at a button nose, etc.

Other theme suggestions:
- rings
- shoes
- floats
- cards
- sails
- school

44

TELEVISION CHANNELS

Instruct a small group of students to pretend that they are performing on television. They may act out a favorite television show, a commercial, a special presentation, or whatever they choose. Let members of the "audience" change the channel periodically. When this happens, the performers must immediately change the theme. For example, a situation comedy could become the news or a game show, etc.

AND THEY'RE OFF!
It's Happy Heifer
breaking out
in front....

SYLLABLE IMPROVISATION

Divide the class into teams of four or five students. Each team is to select a word and divide it into syllables. Then the team may act out each syllable to identify the word.

Examples:
industrial (in dust trial), mistake (mist ache), automobile (auto mobile), porcupine (pork you pine), catalog (cat a log), etc.

cough! cough!

smoke?

MISGUIDED CONVERSATIONS

Instruct two students to discuss two different topics of conversation with one another. Each student is to assume that the other is discussing the same topic. The catch is that the students may never mention the topics! Let the students continue the conversation until the class is able to guess the topics or until enough time has lapsed. Then have another pair of students present another misguided conversation!

Example:

Speaker A - a new bicycle   Speaker B - a new friend

Speaker A: I just got a new one today.
Speaker B: Really, where?
Speaker A: At the store.
Speaker B: The store?
Speaker A: Yes, and it didn't cost a lot, either.
Speaker B: You mean you had to pay? I've never paid for mine.
Speaker A: Where do you get them?
Speaker B: Well, mostly at school.
etc.

Speaker A   Speaker B

LET'S ACT!

Skits, Scenes And Storytelling

STORY CIRCLE

Before beginning this activity, discuss what makes a story interesting. Ask the students to name good action words that could be used in stories and to describe exciting settings for stories. Have the students sit in a circle. Roll a ball to a student and ask that student to begin a story. When that student is ready to stop, he or she may roll the ball to another student who must then continue the story. Students may continue rolling the ball and adding onto the story until the story is complete. Older and more capable students may want to tell the story in rhyme!

DR. KNOW-IT-ALL

Have three students stand side by side before the class. Tell the students that they are collectively to be "Dr. Know-It-All." Members of the "audience" can ask Dr. Know-It-All questions after which each player can say one word until a sentence is completed. The three students may not discuss their answers but must simply reply!

For example:
    Question: "Dr. Know-It-All, who invented school?"
    First Person: "School"
    Second Person: "was"
    Third Person: "invented"
    First Person: "by"
    Second Person: "parents."

STORYTELLING

Have a group of students sit in a circle and tell a story using either words or hand movements. Another group of students may stand behind the circle and do the facial expressions, gestures, and body movements to accompany the story.

And the next thing he knew he had a face full of pie!

FUNNY FAIRY TALES

Let small groups of students work together. Each group may choose a fairy tale and change it in some way by updating it, changing character roles or personalities, adding a surprise ending, etc. Have the groups present their funny fairy tales before the class. Good fairy tales to choose from include *Goldilocks and the Three Bears*, *The Three Little Pigs*, *Little Red Riding Hood*, *Hansel and Gretel*, *Cinderella*, and *Sleeping Beauty*.

Big Bad Wolf
RAP

I'm the Big Bad Wolf
If you know what
I mean
If you don't let me in
I will really cause
a scene.

So hey! Pig Men
You'd better let me in
My tummy sure is
achin'
'Cause I'm in the mood
for bacon!
Yeah!

FEELINGS

Let the students work in small groups. Each group may choose a card on which a feeling is written. The group should create a skit to "illustrate" that feeling. The other students must try to guess what feeling is being portrayed. Choose feelings such as silliness, fear, jealousy, anger, happiness, etc.

COSTUME PLAY

Give each group of students two to four costume pieces such as hats, scarves, boots, jewelry, jackets, etc. Instruct the groups to make up skits around the costumes they have been given.

To the theatah, Dahling.

WHIZBIZZY

Discuss various types of television commercials and what advertisers do to sell products (offer free gifts, coupons, or prizes; use celebrities to advertise; make the consumer think he or she needs or deserves the product; conduct comparison tests and surveys, etc.). Instruct the students to create their own commercials for "Whizbizzy" (a product of their choice). Each commercial should tell what the product is, why it is special, who would buy it, and why they would need it. Let the students present their commercials before the group.

T.V. TIME

Divide the students into small groups. Write each of the following "types" of television programs on an index card: game show, drama, comedy, news show. Let each group draw a card and do a parody of an existing program in that category or make up a new show.

FLOOR PLAN PLAYS

Assign each student a "place" and instruct the student to create the stage for that place on a piece of paper. For example, a "place" could be a schoolroom. The student could identify on paper where the teacher's desk is, where the students sit, where the books, maps and chalkboards are, etc.

SKITS IN THE NEWS

Cut out newspaper headlines and place them in a shoe box. Have each group of students choose a headline and create a skit for that headline to be presented before the class. Students might enjoy contributing headlines, too!

TRAPPED

Divide the class into small groups. Ask each group to act out a scene in which they become trapped in some way. Possible scenes might include an elevator stuck between floors, a bus caught in a traffic jam, a group "snowed in" inside a mountain cabin, etc.

NAME THAT SKIT

Write a list of skit "titles" on the chalkboard. Secretly assign a skit title to each group of students and instruct the group to create a skit for that title. After each group presents its skit, let the class try to name that skit! To make the activity a little more fun and challenging, use skit titles that are similar in theme and write more skit titles on the board than there are groups to participate!

RECIPE SKITS

Write a specific setting, character, emotion, time period (past, present or future), and object on each of several index cards. Let each group of students choose a card and make up a skit including each of the components on the card. Or, assign only a setting, a group of characters or a skit title and have the group supply the other components.

Examples:

1. castle
2. dragon
3. silliness
4. past
5. moat

1. classroom
2. student
3. anger
4. present
5. bubble gum

1. Mars
2. Martian
3. fear
4. future
5. spaceship

1. ship
2. sailor
3. loneliness
4. past
5. raft

1. football field
2. football player
3. excitement
4. present
5. football

1. grocery store
2. small child
3. impatience
4. present
5. grocery cart

1. hospital
2. patient
3. happiness
4. future
5. telephone

1. rooftop
2. chimney sweep
3. contentment
4. past
5. broom

THREE VERY SHORT PLAYS

The Three Little Pigs
The Traveling Musicians
Little Red Riding Hood

THE THREE LITTLE PIGS

Narrator: Once upon a time there were three little pigs who decided to build new homes for themselves.

Pig 1: I'm going to use this big bundle of straw to build a fine house.

Pig 2: I'm going to build my house out of sticks.

Pig 3: These bricks will make a strong house for me.

(The three little pigs pantomime building their houses.)

Narrator: Just as the first little pig was closing the door to his new house, a big bad wolf came walking up the path.

Wolf: Let me in, little pig! Let me in!

Pig 1: Not by the hair on my chinny-chin-chin!

Wolf: Then I'll huff and I'll puff and I'll blow your house down!

(The wolf blows down the straw house and Pig 1 runs to Pig 2's house.)

Narrator: The wolf was very angry that the little pig had escaped, but he knew that the little pig probably had run to his brother's house. So, the wolf ran through the forest until he found the house made of sticks.

Wolf: Let me in, little pigs! Let me in!

Pigs 1 & 2: Not by the hair on our chinny-chin-chins!

Wolf: Then I'll huff and I'll puff and I'll blow your house down!

(The wolf blows down the stick house and both pigs run to Pig 3's house.)

Narrator: Now the wolf was really angry . . . and very hungry! So, he followed the trail through the forest that led to the third pig's brick house. The wolf stormed up to the house and pounded loudly on the door.

Wolf: Let me in, little pigs! Let me in!

Pigs 1, 2 & 3: Not by the hair on our chinny-chin-chins!

Wolf: Then I'll huff and I'll puff and I'll blow your house down!

Narrator: The wolf huffed and puffed and blew and blew until he was exhausted, but he couldn't blow down the brick house.

Wolf: I know what I'll do! I'll slide down the chimney and surprise those little pigs!

(The wolf pantomimes climbing onto the roof.)

Narrator: Well, the three little pigs were quite smart when they put their heads together, and they guessed what the wolf might try to do. So, they built a roaring fire in the fireplace and waited for the wolf to come sliding down the chimney.

(The wolf pantomimes sliding down the chimney.)

Wolf: Ouch! Ouch! Ouch! (The wolf jumps up and grabs the seat of his pants.)

Pig 3: That should teach you not to bother us ever again!

(The wolf runs away yelping in pain.)

Narrator: And the wolf ran away, never to be seen again.

THE END

THE TRAVELING MUSICIANS

Narrator: Once upon a time there was a donkey who was too old to be of use to his master any longer. The donkey decided to go to the city to become a musician. After traveling a short way, the donkey saw a dog lying on the side of the road.

Donkey: Why are you panting, Mr. Dog?

Dog: I'm old and weak and I can't hunt for my master anymore. What shall I do?

Donkey: I'm going to the city to become a great musician. Why don't you join me?

Narrator: So, the dog and the donkey traveled on towards the city. They hadn't gone far when they came upon a little cat.

Donkey: What is the matter with you, little cat? You look so sad.

Cat: I'm too old and frail to catch mice, and my mistress is going to give me away. Meow! Meow! I don't know what to do!

Dog: Come with us to the city. We're going to be great musicians. You meow very well, and so you can sing with us!

Narrator: The cat joined the donkey and the dog on their journey to the city. As they passed a barnyard, they saw a rooster perched on the gate.

Rooster: Cock-a-doodle-doo!

Donkey: My, what a wonderful noise!

Rooster: Well, I don't feel wonderful. My master plans to eat me for dinner on Sunday. What shall I do?

Cat: Come with us to the city.

Dog: We're going to be great musicians. You crow very nicely, and so you can sing with us!

Narrator: So, the rooster joined the merry band on their journey to the city. Before long, it grew dark and the animals became tired and hungry.

Rooster: I see a light in the house over the hill.

(The rooster points to an imaginary house.)

Cat: Let's ask the people in that house if we may spend the night with them.

Dog: Maybe they will offer us some dinner, too.

Narrator: The animals walked to the house and the donkey peered into the window.

Rooster: What do you see, donkey?

Donkey: There are two men sitting at a table. They are eating dinner . . . and there is money everywhere!

Cat: Money?

Donkey: The men have guns, too!

Dog: They must be robbers!

Rooster: How can we get inside the house?

Donkey: I have an idea!

Narrator: The animals made a plan. The donkey stood on his hind legs and the dog and cat stood beside him. Then the rooster flew to the window ledge and they all began to sing.

(The animals sing together: the donkey brays, the dog barks, the cat meows, and the rooster crows.)

Robber 1: Do you hear that? Let's get out of here!

Robber 2: I'm right behind you!

(The robbers exit quickly.)

Donkey: Hurray! They're running away!

Dog: We did it!

(The animals enter the house.)

Cat: We had better return all of this money to the bank in the city tomorrow morning.

Rooster: Look at all of this food. Let's eat!

Narrator: The next morning the animals made their way to the city bank to return the money and they became heroes. The animals stayed to make their home in the city and worked hard to become great musicians!

THE END

LITTLE RED RIDING HOOD

Narrator: Once upon a time there lived a girl named Little Red Riding Hood. She was called this because she liked to wear a bright red cape with a hood that framed her shiny locks of hair. Little Red Riding Hood had a grandmother who lived deep within the forest and whom she visited as often as she could.

Little Red Riding Hood: Poor Grandma isn't feeling well today. I think I'll take her a basket of food.

(Little Red Riding Hood packs a basket of food.)

Narrator: As Little Red Riding Hood walked through the forest, a big bad wolf saw her and stopped her in her path.

Wolf: Well, little girl, where are you going this fine morning?

Little Red Riding Hood: I'm sorry, Mr. Wolf, but I'm not supposed to talk to strangers.

(Little Red Riding Hood walks away from the wolf.)

Narrator: But the big bad wolf did not give up so easily. He followed Little Red Riding Hood through the forest, making sure that he was well hidden by the trees and bushes. When she was almost to her grandmother's house, the wolf ran ahead of her through the woods and went to the back door. Finding the door unlocked, the wolf crept inside, tied up the grandmother and hid her in the closet.

Little Red Riding Hood: (Knocking at the door) Grandma! It's me, Little Red Riding Hood.

Wolf: (Speaking in a high-pitched voice as he throws on a robe and cap of the grandmother's and jumps into her bed) What a nice surprise! Do come in, dear!

Little Red Riding Hood: (Spoken as she hugs the wolf) My, Grandma, what big arms you have!

Wolf: All the better to hug you with, my dear.

Little Red Riding Hood: Oh, Grandma, what large ears you have!

Wolf: All the better to hear you with, my dear.

Little Red Riding Hood: Why, Grandma, what huge eyes you have!

Wolf: All the better to see you with, deary.

Little Red Riding Hood: And Grandma, what big teeth you have!

Wolf: All the better to eat you with!

(The wolf jumps out of bed and tries to grab Little Red Riding Hood. She runs to the closet to hide and finds Grandma escaping from the ropes.)

Grandma: (Hitting the wolf with a broom) Take that, and that, you beast!

Wolf: (Yelping in pain) Help! Help!

Little Red Riding Hood: (Picking up the phone) Hello, police? We have a burglar in our house! Please come quickly!

(The wolf grabs the phone as the grandmother continues hitting him with the broom.)

Wolf: Yes, hurry! I need help!

(All of the players freeze except the narrator.)

Narrator: The police arrived quickly and arrested the big bad wolf, and Little Red Riding Hood and her grandmother lived happily ever after!

THE END

PUTTING ON A PLAY

Selecting, Writing And Directing A Play

SELECTING A PLAY

1. Select a play suitable for the age, maturity level and capabilities of the students.

2. Consider the length of the play itself. Plays for primary students generally should not exceed thirty to forty minutes.

3. Choose a play that is entertaining as well as intellectually stimulating and educational in some way. The play should have a strong plot supported by interesting characters, dialogue and action.

4. Select a play with characters, costumes and set specifications which meet the capabilities of your budget and resources.

5. Write to play companies and request their catalogs which list and describe their available plays. Refer to the play companies and play magazine on page 65 and check the public library for books and magazines containing additional resources (see the bibliography on page 79).

6. Consider the option of writing the play yourself or having your students help write the play. This will eliminate the necessity of paying royalties and will allow you to control the number of characters, set demands and costuming.

WRITING A PLAY

1. Choose a theme. Consider the ages and capabilities of the students as well as the time of year and occasion when the play is to be presented. Decide whether or not the play will teach a moral.

2. Determine the number of characters you will need.

3. Consider the place where you will rehearse and perform the play — a large stage, a small room, the outdoors, etc. This will determine the possibilities of the play.

4. Consider how much time you will have to produce the play. The length of rehearsals should have a bearing on the length of the play.

5. Find out the limitations of your budget for costumes and the set. If you have an adequate budget and sewing volunteers, the characters can wear fancy costumes. If not, representational costumes are an option (a cardboard crown can designate the king), or characters may be "outfitted" with regular "street" clothes. Sets may be as simple as a chair and table or as elaborate as a painted background.

6. Write an outline of the story plot and then flesh out the dialogue. After reviewing and revising the script, type the final copy which may be reproduced and distributed to the characters.

RESOURCES FOR PLAYS

Play Companies

Baker's Play Publishing Company
100 Chauncy St.
Boston, MA 02111

Coach House Press, Inc.
Box 458
Morton, IL 60053

Contemporary Drama Service
885 Elkton Dr.
Colorado Springs, CO 80907

The Dramatic Publishing Company
311 Washington Street
Woodstock, IL 60098

Eldridge Publishing Company
Drawer 216
Franklin, OH 45005

Samuel French, Inc.
45 W. 25th Street
New York, NY 10010

Pioneer Drama Service
2171 South Colorado Blvd.
Box 22555
Denver, CO 80222

Play Magazine

Plays, The Drama Magazine for Young People
120 Boylston
Boston, MA 02116

NOTES TO THE DIRECTOR

1 *The Prompt Book*
After you have chosen a play, make a prompt book. Place the pages of the script in a three-ring notebook. If the pages are small, glue them to notebook paper. Write all of your notes concerning cues, stage movements, instructions, etc. in the margins of the prompt book (see *Blocking The Script* below). This will be your one and only reference!

2 *Blocking The Script*
The prompt book should include blocking, or the planned stage movements of the actors. Draw a small diagram of the stage at the top of each page to show where the characters are located on the stage at this point in the scene. You may find it helpful to use buttons or coins to "position" the characters before drawing the diagram. Blocking may be changed several times during rehearsals, so always use a pencil!

Note each character's movements beside his or her lines of dialogue. For example:

Mary - Really, John, what are you doing?   X UR to J (cross upright to John)

(See page 72 for stage areas and terms.)

Also note stage "business" in the margins of the prompt book. "Business" includes eating, reading, knitting, and any other kind of activity that does not involve movement from one place to another.

3 *Character Analysis*
Write a character analysis for each character in the play. Each character analysis should be one to two paragraphs describing the character's personality, mannerisms, interests, relationships with others, etc. (See page 76.) Give each character analysis to the appropriate cast member to use in developing his or her character.

4 *The Setting*
Examine the setting of the play. It is usually best to keep the set as simple as possible. A set may consist of borrowed furniture or a simple backdrop made of butcher paper. The set should be completed at least one week before the performances begin in order to allow the cast to rehearse with the set in place.

5 *Lighting, Sound and Props*
Lighting helps to make the action on the stage visible. It also can establish the mood and time of day. Select someone to be in charge of working the lights.

Sound effects such as a ringing telephone or a wind storm show that life exists beyond the set. All sound effects should stir the imagination of the audience and complement the style of the play. Sound can indicate an action, show a locale, or reinforce character. Tape all of the sound effects in advance and select a person to be in charge of playing the sound effects at the appropriate times during the performances.

Before the first rehearsal, make a list of all of the props needed for the play. Then assign specific props to each cast member. Or, designate a prop committee to be responsible for securing all of the props. Assign one or more persons to be in charge of putting props on the stage at the appropriate times during the play. If you will be changing the set during the play, a set crew may be responsible for props as well.

The persons responsible for lighting, sound and props will need cue sheets — pages of the script marked to signal the crew when to change the lighting, play a sound effect or place a prop. Each of these persons will need to be present for the last week of rehearsals.

6 *Costumes*
Costumes help to define a character's personality as well as to show time and place. Assign specific costume pieces to the cast members or designate a costumes committee. Thrift shops are great places to find wonderful costumes at bargain prices. If you have the resources, a sewing committee can be invaluable!

7 Makeup

The lighting to be used during the play will determine the kind of makeup the characters should wear. If you will not be using lights, the actors will need only character makeup — simple features added to help to identify or define a character (such as a moustache for the villain and round rosy cheeks for the damsel in distress). If you will be using lights, the actors will need to wear stage makeup to prevent their faces from appearing washed out.

The application of stage makeup is very important. First, cover the face and neck with a small amount of cold cream or baby oil. Next, apply the base by "dotting" it on and then blending. To apply rouge, carefully blend it into the foundation. To show age, use an eyebrow pencil to follow the actor's natural lines or to create lines where they are needed. This is less time consuming than highlighting, which involves using a light makeup on prominent areas of the face (chin, cheekbones, etc.) and a darker shade in the shadows (indentation of cheeks, under eyes, etc.). After all of the makeup has been applied, powder the face to set the makeup and remove the shine.

To age the hair, first apply cold cream or baby oil and then spray or powder the hair to create the desired effect.

8 Auditions

There are many factors to consider when casting the characters of a play. Physical build, voice pitch and volume, acting ability, and personality are major considerations. Reliability and maturity are also extremely important characteristics to look for when choosing cast members. Always remember, acting ability is more easily taught than discipline.

Use the audition form on page 74 when holding an audition. If you have a large audition, assign each student an audition number and write this number on an index card to be pinned to the student's clothing. Have each student read selected portions of the script as well as improvise. For example, if a student is auditioning for the role of Santa Claus, ask him to "become" Santa — to walk like Santa, to have an imaginary conversation with a child like Santa would, etc. As each student auditions, make notes such as these:

Audition Number	Sex	Voice	Script Reading	Improvisation
#1	F	strong	o.k.	excellent

You also may want to include a physical description of each student in your notes to help you in casting the roles.

Necessary supplies for an audition:

● scripts
● audition pages (specific scenes from the play)
● actor's contract and rules (to post so that the students can see what they will be asked to sign if they are chosen — see *Rehearsal Schedule and Contracts*)
● index cards and straight pins (for audition numbers)
● clipboard
● notebook paper
● pencils
● masking tape (to mark the places on the stage where the students are to stand and to post the audition notices, actor's contract and rules)

Post audition notices two weeks before the audition. Decide in advance whether or not to allow spectators to attend the audition. Closed auditions often help to ease the nervousness and self-consciousness of students. Try to make your cast selections as soon after the audition is over as possible. This will allow you to review your notes while they are still clear in your mind as well as to post the chosen cast members soon after the audition to satisfy anxious students.

Try to involve the students who auditioned but were not chosen to be in the play in other aspects of the play such as costuming, set design and construction, props, lighting, sound effects, etc. These students will be enthusiastic and will feel good about being able to participate in the production of the play.

9 *Rehearsal Schedule and Contracts*
Outline a rehearsal schedule before holding the audition. Generally, six weeks is ample time to produce a fairly large production. If you are planning a shorter and less involved play, adjust the schedule as necessary.

Example: Week 1   Blocking
               Week 2   Lines Memorized
               Week 3   Props Gathered/Sound Effects Recorded
               Week 4   Costumes Made or Gathered
               Week 5   Set Complete/Dress Rehearsals
               Week 6   Performances

Make sure that everyone in the cast has a copy of the rehearsal schedule and actor's contract (page 75) before the rehearsals begin. This will help to assure that the cast members take rehearsals seriously.

Explain all "rules" at the first rehearsal. It is a good idea to type the rules and leave spaces at the bottom of the page for the student's and parent's signatures. Give each cast member a copy of the rules and ask the student to read and sign the paper and to have his or her parent(s) do the same. Make a list of rules such as those below, adding others as necessary and deleting those that do not apply to your situation.

---

1. It is the responsibility of each student to get to all rehearsals and performances on time.
2. Students will be excused from rehearsals only in the case of illness. A written excuse and parent's signature will be required.
3. All lines must be memorized by the second week of rehearsals.
4. Each student is expected to work at least two hours on costumes, the set, and/or props.
5. If any of these rules is broken, the director has the right to drop a student from the play.

_____   _____
            Student   Parent

---

10 *Publicity*
If the play is intended to be a money-raiser for your school or organization, contact local newspapers and radio and television stations to inquire about free or inexpensive advertising. Involve the students in designing posters and flyers to distribute to local libraries and store merchants. You may want to sell tickets in advance or simply charge at the door. Form a committee of parents to be in charge of tickets and ticket sales.

If the play is not intended to raise money, invite other classes and/or the entire school as well as children's clubs and organizations to attend the performances. Nothing enhances self-concept more than performing in front of peers!

STAGE AREAS AND TERMS

Stage Areas

Up Right	(UR)
Right	(R)
Down Right	(DR)
Up Center	(UC)
Center	(C)
Down Center	(DC)
Up Left	(UL)
Left	(L)
Down Left	(DL)

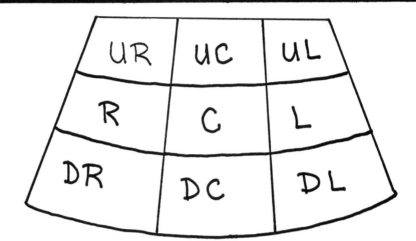

Types of Staging

Proscenium — the most common arrangement of theaters, school gyms, and assembly halls — a stage in front of the audience, sometimes framed by an arch and a curtain; lends itself well to large set pieces, elaborate backdrops, and plays with many scene changes

Thrust — the situation often encountered in classrooms and used in many theaters, with the audience situated on two or three sides of the acting area; advantages are closer contact between the actors and audience and a more "realistic" feel (requires more imaginative blocking so that one side of the audience is not left out)

Arena or Round — an acting area with the audience on all four sides, a very intimate arrangement; eliminates the possibility of large set pieces, scene changes, and backdrops (requires careful blocking and more experienced actors)

Blocking Terms

Block — (of directors) to direct the movement and placement of actors on the stage; (of actors) to block the audience's view — one actor may block another actor by standing in front of that actor, and an actor may block himself by holding an object in front of his face or by turning away from the audience

Business — any kind of activity that does not involve movement from one place to another

Counter — a move in the opposite direction made by an upstage actor when an actor downstage crosses in front of him or her

Cross (X) — to move from one place to another on the stage

Downstage — towards the audience or the front of the stage

Open Up — to turn and face the audience

Stage Left — towards the left of the stage (actor's perspective)

Stage Right — towards the right of the stage (actor's perspective)

Upstage — away from the audience or toward the back of the stage

APPENDIX

AUDITION FORM

Name _____ Audition Number _____

Address _____

_____

_____

Phone Number _____

Interested in:
makeup   _____
costumes   _____
scenery   _____
props   _____
sound effects   _____
lighting   _____
publicity   _____

Costume information:
height   _____
weight   _____
dress and/or
    pants size _____
shirt size   _____
shoe size   _____

Roles interested in:

1.

2.

List any conflicts you might have with rehearsals (team practices, appointments, etc.):

ACTOR'S CONTRACT

I, _____ , agree to attend all
 (name)

rehearsals for the play _____ .
 (name of play)

The rehearsals have been set for _____
 (days of week and times)

from _____ to _____ .
 (date of 1st rehearsal)   (date of last rehearsal)

If I miss a rehearsal other than because of illness, I understand that I may be dropped from the play. I agree to uphold all of my responsibilities and follow the director's instructions.

_____
Student's signature

_____
Parent's signature

CHARACTER ANALYSIS FORM

Character: _____

General Analysis (personality, mannerisms, interests, relationships with others, etc.):

_____
_____
_____
_____
_____
_____
_____
_____
_____
_____
_____
_____
_____
_____

Actor/Actress To Play This Character: _____

Actor's/Actress's Notes:

_____
_____
_____
_____
_____
_____
_____
_____

GENERAL MOVEMENT RULES FOR ACTORS

1. Never turn your back to the audience unless an exit requires it or the director requests it.
2. Always make forward gestures with the upstage hand.
3. Always make backward gestures with the downstage hand.
4. Always kneel on the downstage knee.
5. Move only when you are speaking unless instructed to do otherwise. If you have nothing to do, stand still.
6. Take your first step on your upstage foot when you make a cross.

CUES FOR ACTORS AND DIRECTORS

- Always remember:
   diction
   projection
   energy
   pace
   posture

- Pick up cues

- Memorize lines and cues
- Be attentive in the wings
- Do not upstage other actors
- Pay attention to other actors
- Keep business and movements clear
- Remember the little old lady sitting in the back row!

BIBLIOGRAPHY OF GOOD STORY BOOKS, POETRY BOOKS AND PLAY BOOKS

Story Books

Balian, Lorna. *Humbug Rabbit.* Abingdon Press, 1974.

Brown, Marcia. *Stone Soup.* Macmillan, 1986.

Freeman, Don. *Corduroy.* Penguin, 1976.

Gramatky, Hardie. *Little Toot.* Putnam Publishing Group, 1978.

Kellogg, Steven. *A Rose for Pinkerton.* Dial Books for Young Readers, 1984.

Krauss, Ruth. *Leo the Late Bloomer.* Harper & Row Jr. Books, 1987.

Lionni, Leo. *Frederick.* Alfred A. Knopf, Inc., 1987.

Lobel, Arnold. *Fables.* Harper & Row Jr. Books, 1983.

Mayer, Mercer. *There's A Nightmare in My Closet.* Dial Books for Young Readers, 1976.

McClosky, Robert. *Blueberries for Sal.* Penguin, 1976.

Milne, A. A. *Winnie the Pooh.* Dell, 1970.

Peet, Bill. *Huge Harold.* Houghton Mifflin, 1982.

Sendak, Maurice. *Where the Wild Things Are.* Harper & Row Jr. Books, 1984.

Schwartz, Alvin. *Scary Stories to Tell in the Dark.* Harper & Row Jr. Books, 1981.

Slobodkina, Esphyr. *Caps for Sale.* Harper & Row Jr. Books, 1987.

Steig, William. *Sylvester and the Magic Pebble.* Windmill Books, 1969.

Thurber, James. *Many Moons.* Harcourt Brace Jovanovich, 1943.

Viorst, Judith. *Alexander and the Terrible, Horrible, No Good, Very Bad Day.* Macmillan, 1987.

Poetry Books

Blishen, Edward. *Oxford Book of Poetry for Children.* P. Bedrick Books, 1984.

Cole, William. *A Boy Named Mary Jane and Other Silly Verse.* Avon, 1979.

Cole, William, ed. *An Arkful of Animals: Poems for the Very Young.* Houghton Mifflin, 1978.

Conyers, DeWitt. *Animal Poems for Children.* Western Publishing, 1982.

Emrich, Duncan. *The Nonsense Book of Riddles, Rhymes, Tongue Twisters, Puzzles and Jokes from American Folklore.* Four Winds, 1970.

Lobel, Arnold. *Whiskers and Rhymes.* Greenwillow, 1985.

Nash, Ogden. *Custard and Company.* Little, Brown & Co., 1980.

Ness, Evaline. *Amelia Mixed the Mustard and Other Poems.* Scribner, 1975.

Prelutsky, Jack. *The New Kid on the Block.* Greenwillow, 1984.

Prelutsky, Jack. *Nightmares: Poems to Trouble Your Sleep.* Greenwillow, 1976.

Silverstein, Shel. *A Light in the Attic.* Harper & Row Jr. Books, 1981.

Silverstein, Shel. *Where the Sidewalk Ends: Poems and Drawings.* Harper & Row Jr. Books, 1974.

Play Books

Alexander, Sue. *Small Plays for Special Days.* Houghton Mifflin, 1976.

Alexander, Sue. *Whatever Happened to Uncle Albert?* Houghton Mifflin, 1980.

Bradley, Virginia. *Holidays on Stage: A Festival of Special-Occasion Plays.* Dodd, 1981.

Bradley, Virginia. *Is There an Actor in the House? Dramatic Material From Pantomime to Play.* Dodd, 1985.

George, Richard R. *Charlie and the Chocolate Factory: A Play.* (Adapted from Roald Dahl's story *Charlie and the Chocolate Factory.*) Penguin, 1983.

Harris, Aurand and Coleman A. Jennings. *Plays Children Love: A Treasury of Contemporary and Classic Plays for Children.* Doubleday, 1981.

Kamerman, Sylvia E., ed. *Children's Plays From Favorite Stories.* Plays, Inc., 1985.

Kamerman, Sylvia E. *Holiday Plays Round the Year.* Plays, Inc., 1983.